Collins

Tommy Donbavand

1 Friends

Mark Tenby hasn't been at our school for long, but he's already my best friend. I've got lots of other friends, of course, but they just don't get me in the same way that Mark does. We both support the same football team, both like the same computer games, and we both watch the same TV shows.

Some of the other kids at school say that Mark's a bit weird. He isn't really; he just does a few things that make him stand out. Like the way he never comes into the dining room at lunchtime. Mark always takes his packed lunch to a quiet corner of the playground and eats his sandwiches there, alone.

I asked him why, once, and he just said that the dining room is too noisy for him. Fair enough, I suppose. And once he's finished his lunch, he always comes and finds me so we can have a game of football. I don't know what the others are moaning about.

Mark's great at football – better than me, in fact – but I don't mind because he always makes sure that we play on the same team.

One lunchtime, we'd managed to get enough kids together for a game of six-a-side, and Mark had just scored a goal. I helped, though: I was the one that crossed the ball to him, setting him up for the shot. It was a belter, just skimming inside the pile of school bags that was the left goalpost. One–nil to us!

"Nice pass there, Al!" he said, patting me on the back.

We were just about to kick off again when Mark's phone rang. I knew it was his, because his ring tone is the theme to our favourite TV show. He pulled it out of his pocket and checked the number.

"It's Mother," he said with a smile. "I'll be back in a minute." Then he jogged over to the side of the playground to answer the call.

"He's always on the phone to 'Mother'!" teased Omar, one of the boys on the other team. "How posh are they? And she can't even go for a few hours without ringing her ickle baby Marky-Warky!"

The other kids laughed, which I thought
was a bit cruel, but it was the truth. Mark's
mum rang him at least three times a day – and
he always called her "Mother". You weren't
supposed to have your phone switched on in
school, but Mark always seemed to get away
with it. The teachers never caught him.

"Sorry about that," grinned Mark as he ran back over to us. "You ready?"

"We've been ready for ages!" said Omar.

That was a lie – Mark had only been a few minutes.

We kicked off again, but now Omar seemed to have it in for Mark. He started tackling him really hard, and shoving him out of the way whenever anyone passed him the ball. Then he deliberately tripped Mark up as he was about to score again.

"Penalty!" shouted the other kids on my team.

But I didn't. Mark was holding his knee, and I was worried that he'd hurt himself. I ran over and crouched down beside him. His trousers were torn, and I expected to see loads of blood where he'd cut himself – but there was none of that. Mark's skin was ripped back and, inside his knee, there was a long, metal bar and loads of coloured wires. There was even a tiny circuit board, like the ones you get in computers.

"What's wrong with your leg?" I asked, staring.

Before he could reply, there was a BEEP as Mark got a text message. He pulled out his phone, and I peeked over his shoulder at the screen.

The message said:

RETURN HOME NOW. MOTHER.

Without saying another word, Mark jumped to his feet, ran across the playground and out of school.

2 Mark's House

I didn't know what to do at first. Only the Year 11 kids are allowed out of school at lunchtime, and I knew I'd get into lots of trouble if I went after Mark. We had ICT with Mr Prime after lunch, and he'd go mad if I didn't show up.

But Mark was my best mate, and something was badly wrong, so I found some courage from somewhere and ran out of the gates after him.

The street outside the school was empty, but I guessed that Mark would have headed for home, and I set off in that direction. I'd never been to his house before, but I knew where it was as my nan used to live in the same street.

As I ran, I began to wonder what it was I'd seen inside Mark's knee.

It certainly wasn't flesh and bone. Maybe Mark had a robotic leg? Maybe he'd been in some sort of accident, and he'd had his leg cut off, and the doctors had given him a bionic one? That would certainly explain why he was so good at football; there wasn't a goalkeeper in our year that could stop his shots.

But then why hadn't Mark told me about it before? If I had a cool robotic knee, he'd be the first person I'd tell about it.

I got to Mark's house and rang the bell, but there was no answer.

I shouted through the letter box. "Mark! It's me, Al!"

Still no reply.

I checked my watch. If I left now, I could just get back to class in time for the bell, and I might get away with leaving the school grounds. But I couldn't do that. I had to check that Mark was OK.

Then I found an open window at the side
of the house. I called again. There was still no
answer, so I climbed inside. Even though it was
the middle of the day, all the curtains were
closed, and the house was in darkness.

Feeling my way along the wall, I found
a doorway and peered into the dim room
beyond. It was the kitchen, but it was
deserted. I kept going, aiming for what looked
like another door further on.

"Mark?" I called again. I was getting nervous now.

I grasped the handle, pulled the door open and slipped into this new room. It was even darker than the others. I felt along the wall for a light switch, found one and flicked it on. Then – I froze!

3 Mark Tenby

Mark was standing with his back against the wall. His eyes were wide open, but he didn't seem to be awake. Wires ran from all over his body to a computer that sat on a table beside him. Numbers flashed all over the screen, and there was something that looked like one of those heart-rate monitors you see in hospitals. But that wasn't the worst of it ...

There were three other Marks in the room, each identical to my best mate, and each linked up to a PC.

4 Face the Truth

I stared at the four identical Marks in horror, trying to work out what was going on. And then I noticed the labels above the four, silent boys ...

My friend – the one with the ripped trousers and damaged leg – was Mark 10B. Of course! Mark Tenby! But why were there three identical copies of him? And why were they all standing still and looking so strange ...

A phone rang and I nearly jumped out of my skin. It was the theme tune to our favourite TV show again. I pulled the phone out of Mark's pocket and looked at the screen. It said "Mother". Maybe Mark's mum could tell me what was going on. So I answered the call.

But there wasn't a person on the other end of the phone. It was another computer. All I could hear was a screeching sound, with lots of bleeps and bloops mixed in. I couldn't make any sense of it – but that didn't mean that Mark would have the same problem ...

I held the phone up to his ear, and heard
a fizzing sound. I looked down in amazement
to see that his damaged knee was beginning
to repair itself! Sparks flew as the broken wires
fused back together, and new computer chips
slid into place on the tiny circuit board.

Then the flap of loose skin mended itself, and finally the hole in his school trousers stitched itself up. Mark hadn't been getting phone calls from his mum at school – he'd been getting upgrades!

I was pretty excited to have worked it out, and I guess I wasn't looking at what I was doing. I must have pressed the phone a bit too hard because I felt his ear shift backwards slightly. There was a CLICK and a WHIRR – and then Mark's entire face hinged open.

5 Mr Prime

The inside of Mark's head was a mass of flashing lights and circuit boards. It wasn't just his leg that was computerised – he was a robot!

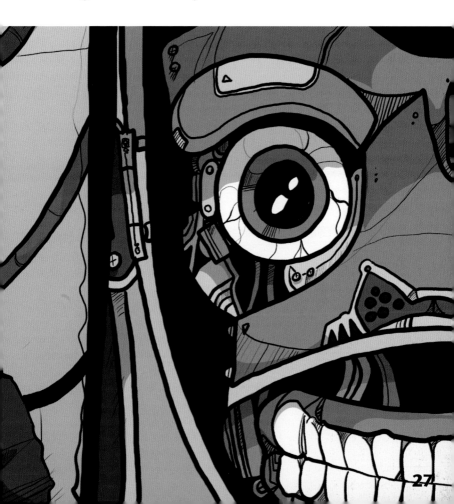

Now I was terrified. I ran out of the room and back to the open window. The other kids at school were right: Mark was weird, and so were his robotic copies. There was no way I was going to hang around until they woke up and found me there.

I ran all the way back to school and crashed into my ICT class. I didn't care that I was late, and that I would get into trouble for leaving school at lunchtime. Mr Prime was a computer teacher and, if anyone knew what to do, it would be him.

"Mr Prime!" I yelled. "Mark Tenby is a robot, and there are three more like him hidden in his house!"

I expected everyone in the classroom to laugh. It sounded pretty silly even to me, and I'd just seen it for myself. But the kids just stared at me in silence.

Mr Prime left his desk and came over to me. "Al?" he said. "Al Farate? Calm down. Tell me what happened."

It all came out at once.

"Mark hurt his leg at lunch, but instead of blood there were wires, sir!" I said. "I followed him home and found three more Marks just like him. And then Mark's face fell off!"

Mr Prime smiled a funny smile. "Do you mean like this?"

He reached up to the side of his head and pressed his left ear back. There was a CLICK and a WHIRR, and my ICT teacher removed his own face. Again, there was nothing but spinning gears and flashing lights.

I wanted to scream. I wanted everyone to scream, and I glanced over Mr Prime's shoulder to see why everyone was so calm.

CLICK! WHIRR! CLICK! WHIRR! CLICK! WHIRR!

Everyone else in the class – the kids I'd known since we started primary school together – clicked open their own faces.

What was going on?!

Then a phone rang. *My* phone!

"Don't you think you'd better answer that?" asked Mr Prime.

His voice sounded metallic, and I couldn't tell which part of the inside of his robotic head it came from.

Fingers trembling, I pulled the phone from my pocket and stared at the screen. The name of the caller was "Mother".

Slowly, I raised the phone up and pressed it hard to my ear.

CLICK! WHIRR!

Test subject: ALPHA 8

MOTHER'S NOTES: The cyber unit known as Al Farate believed he was a real human being until the age of 14. He was good, but now he knows he is not human, he is no longer suitable for the Earth invasion force. Wipe the unit's memory and reset to standard settings.

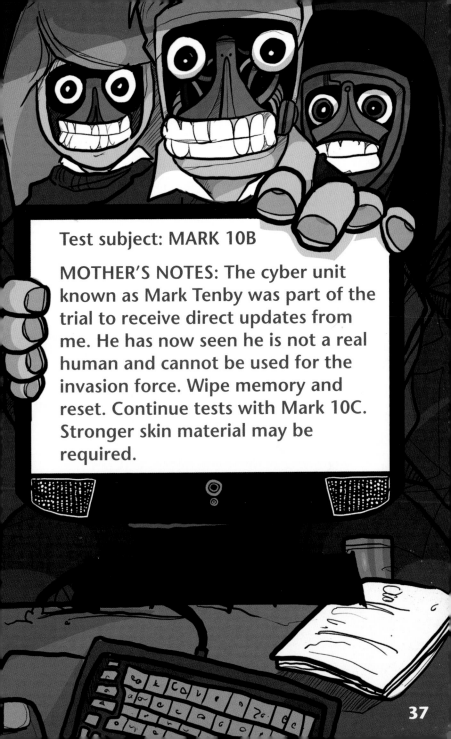

Test subject: MARK 10B

MOTHER'S NOTES: The cyber unit known as Mark Tenby was part of the trial to receive direct updates from me. He has now seen he is not a real human and cannot be used for the invasion force. Wipe memory and reset. Continue tests with Mark 10C. Stronger skin material may be required.

Reader challenge

Word hunt

1 On page 9, find a verb that means "smiled broadly".

2 On page 13, find a noun that means "bravery".

3 On page 28, find an adjective that means "very scared".

Story sense

4 Why did Omar tease Mark? (page 7)

5 What did Al see when Mark tripped up and why was he surprised? (page 11)

6 Why do you think Al decided to climb into Mark's house, even though it was dark inside? (page 17)

7 What did it really mean when "Mother" was calling Mark's phone? (page 22)

8. How does Al find out he is a robot himself? (pages 34–35)

Your views

9. Did you enjoy the story? Give reasons.

10. At what point in the story did you realise Mark was a robot? What clues were there?

Spell it

With a partner, look at these words and then cover them up.

- setting
- skimming
- spinning

Take it in turns for one of you to read the words aloud. The other person has to try and spell each word. Check your answers, then swap over.

Try it

With a partner, discuss what you would do if you found out your friend was a robot. Would you do what Al did? How would you act? Who would you tell? How would you feel?

William Collins's dream of knowledge for all began with the publication of his first book in 1819. A self-educated mill worker, he not only enriched millions of lives, but also founded a flourishing publishing house. Today, staying true to this spirit, Collins books are packed with inspiration, innovation and practical expertise. They place you at the centre of a world of possibility and give you exactly what you need to explore it.

Collins. Freedom to teach.

Published by Collins Education
An imprint of HarperCollins*Publishers*
77-85 Fulham Palace Road
Hammersmith
London
W6 8JB

Browse the complete Collins Education catalogue at **www.collins.co.uk**

Text © Tommy Donbavand 2014
Illustrations by Nic Brennan © HarperCollins*Publishers* 2014

Series consultants: Alan Gibbons and Natalie Packer

10 9 8 7 6 5 4 3 2 1
ISBN 978-0-00-746473-9

British Library Cataloguing in Publication Data.
A catalogue record for this publication is available from the British Library.

Commissioned by Catherine Martin
Edited by Sue Chapple
Project-managed by Lucy Hobbs and Caroline Green
Illustration management by Tim Satterthwaite
Proofread by Hugh Hillyard-Parker
Typeset by Jouve India, Ltd
Cover design by Paul Manning
Production by Emma Roberts
Printed and bound in China by South China Printing Co.

Acknowledgements

The publishers would like to thank the students and teachers of the following schools for their help in trialling the Read On series:

Park View Academy, London
Southfields Academy, London
St Mary's College, Hull
Queensbury School, Queensbury, Bradford
Ormiston Six Villages Academy, Chichester